Doug the Waterbug's First Christmas

It was Christmas Eve day

All the critters came out to play

From far and wide

None wanted to stay inside

Not local boy Sam

The fresh water clam

Not a gal called Tess

All the way from Lock Ness

Doug could see

They came from land, air and sea

A magical day

For all to come play

The gateway guarded by Irwin

He is a sea urchin

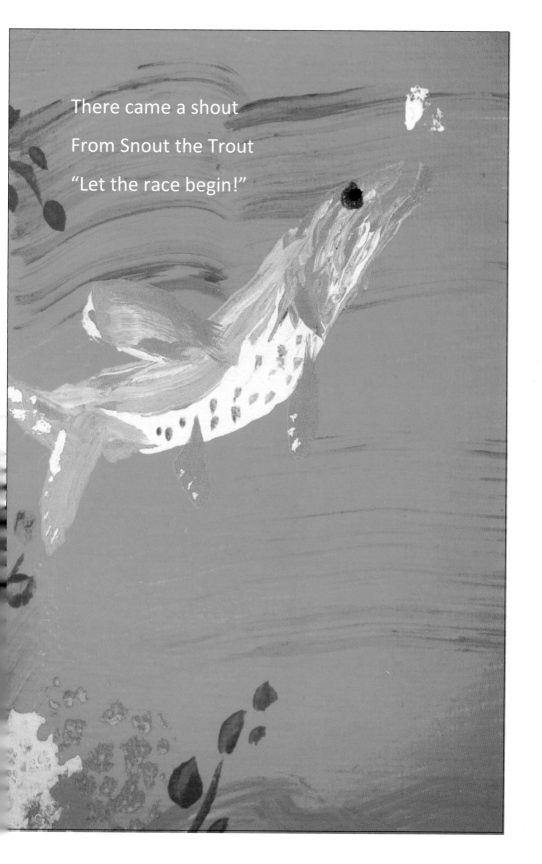

There came a shout

From Snout the Trout

"Let the race begin!"

Many joined in

Racing with legs and fins

They crossed

A red hat someone lost

Snout darted to the end

Announcing who would win

With a one, two, three, go!

Racing through ice and snow

Some glided in water blue

Others just flew

It didn't matter who won

Just having Christmas fun

Snout shouted the names

Finishing the racing game

Doug the water bug!

Spike the pike!

Blake the snake didn't care

Sticking his tongue in the air

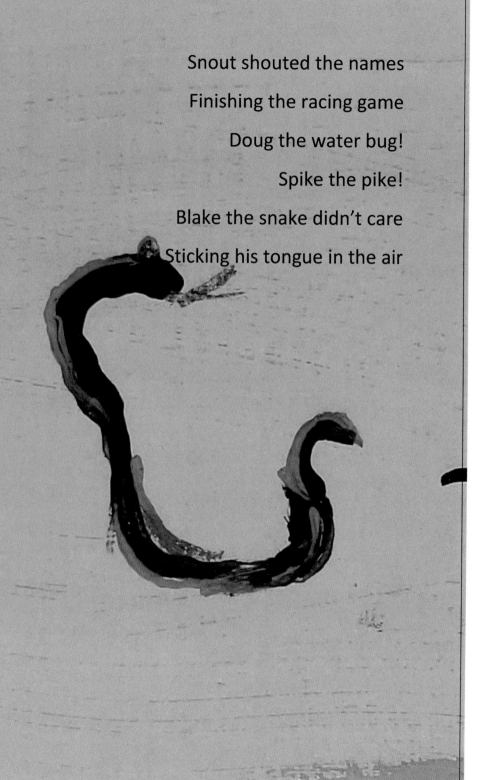

Howie the sea cowie

Could have been next

But he took a bend

To say hi to a friend

Lord the fish with a sword

Edged out Myrtle the turtle

She thought it was a blast

Waddling in last

Waiting,

Doug spotted her skating

There was Missy

Doug's older sissy

She was spinning

And grinning

"Today is for you"

"first Christmas true!"

As they played on

He could hear their song:

Our greatest joy

Not getting a toy

Helping tonight

With Saint Nick's flight

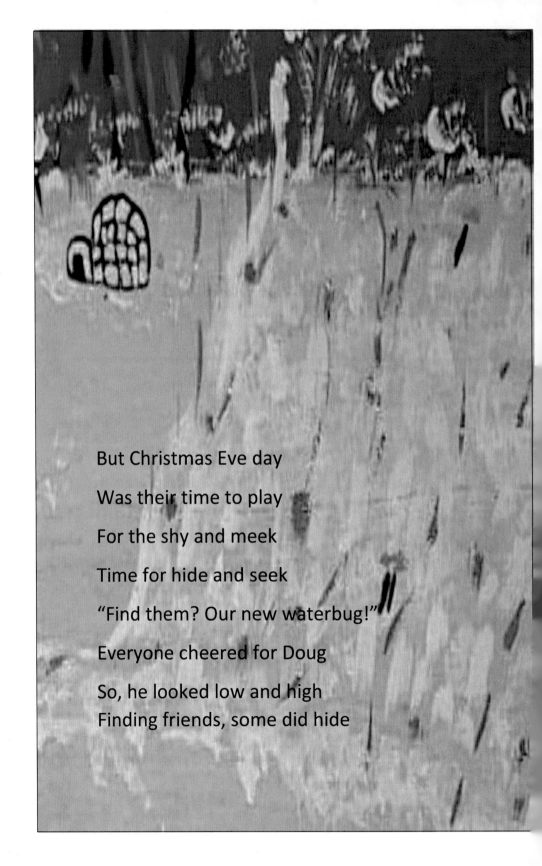

But Christmas Eve day

Was their time to play

For the shy and meek

Time for hide and seek

"Find them? Our new waterbug!"

Everyone cheered for Doug

So, he looked low and high
Finding friends, some did hide

It was fun sport

Looking carefully at the ice fort

Almost missed Flo

 the Doe

Too excited, she had to peek

Sitting still was no easy feat

Feel a breeze

Swooping into the trees

It was a clue indeed

Follow the wind's lead

His eyes did their best

Spotting a nest

Al the red cardinal

Wasn't really at rest

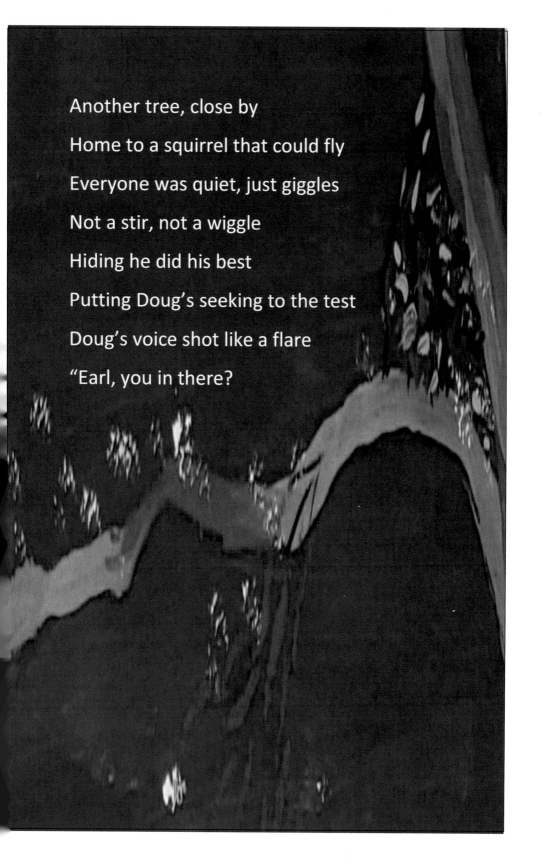

Another tree, close by

Home to a squirrel that could fly

Everyone was quiet, just giggles

Not a stir, not a wiggle

Hiding he did his best

Putting Doug's seeking to the test

Doug's voice shot like a flare

"Earl, you in there?

Shouts came from the crowd

"You found him! We are so proud!"

More friends to find

Leave nobody behind

Looking far beyond

Trees at the edge of the pond

There was Lair

The black bear

Doug was getting good

Finding hiders in the woods

He looked twice

Finding some under the ice

Doug knelt to peer

A friend was near

Of course

Melton the sea horse

Many had their spell

Hiding quite well

A sudden itch

Caused a hider to twitch

And there was Sam

The fresh water Clam

Did you know?

There are three to go!

It took some time

To figure this one out

Creeping slowly

Doug gave a shout

It's the other Doug

He's a water slug!

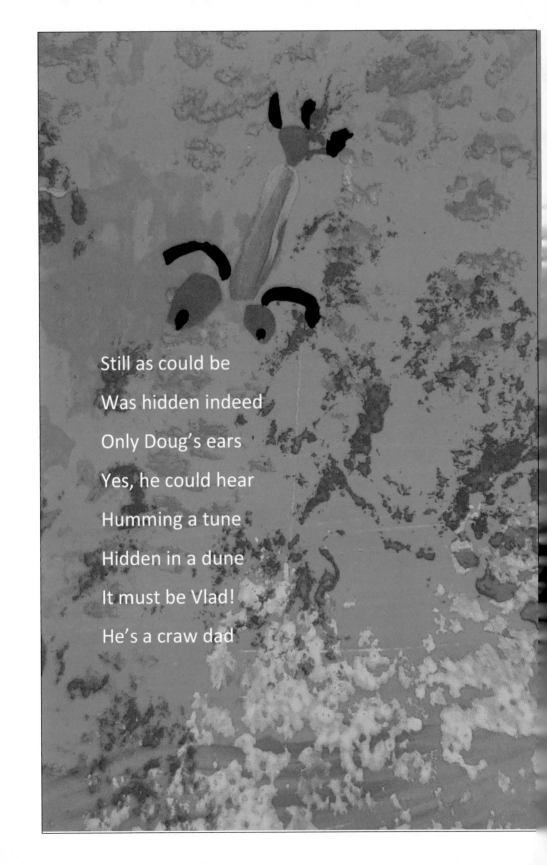

Still as could be

Was hidden indeed

Only Doug's ears

Yes, he could hear

Humming a tune

Hidden in a dune

It must be Vlad!

He's a craw dad

She looked like an igloo

But Doug knew

And with a hurdle

He caught Myrtle the turtle

Hide and seek was done

Time for new fun

With a shout

Earl flew out

Shaking all the trees

Sending snow in the breeze

Can't let Earl have all the fun

Thus, the snow fight begun

Larry the canary grew bold

Not fearing the cold

Dropping snow bombs galore

At the icy floor

Bo the crow joined in

Dive bombing with a spin

Snow exploded like a spark

Each time Bo hit the mark

As the fort got pelted

Snow dust quickly melted

Such a warm day

Perfect for play

Dox the fox got the worst

Of all the snow burst

With a toothy grin

"Counterattack begins!"

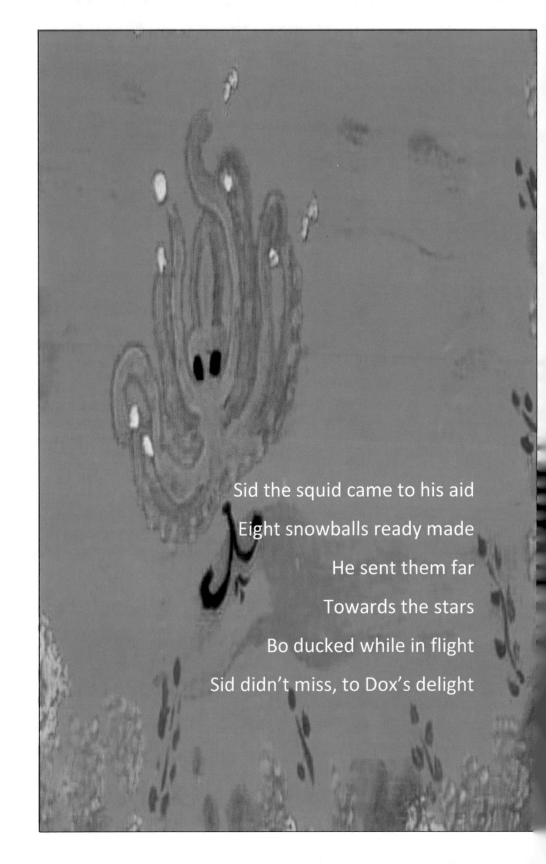

Sid the squid came to his aid

Eight snowballs ready made

He sent them far

Towards the stars

Bo ducked while in flight

Sid didn't miss, to Dox's delight

Sid's arms were strong

Thrown so long

To someone else

The best throw did belong

With a whip of her neck

That's Tess

Right at Earl

Who started this mess

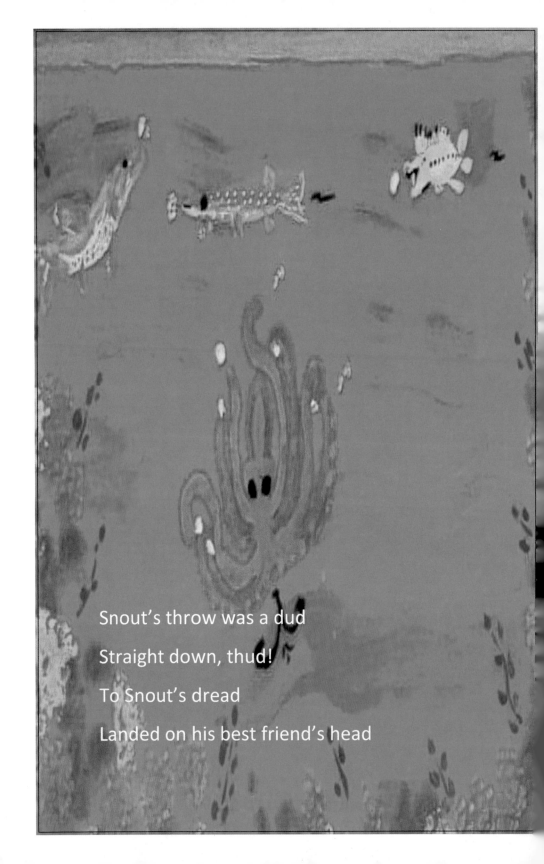

Snout's throw was a dud

Straight down, thud!

To Snout's dread

Landed on his best friend's head

A chase broke out below

Circling each other with snow

Howie, Goldie, Belly and Gail

She's the killer whale

Doug watched with bliss

As they all threw and missed

Where did that magical day go?

So much fun in the snow

It would be a thrill

Just to make time stand still

Playing with friends, old and new

But the moon gave his cue

Winking, he said,

"Saint Nicholas' time, so off to bed!"

Friends said their goodbyes

Sissy took Doug by the hand

Many went home across the land

Others swimming through Irwin's gateway

All said "We'll be back next year to play"

Winged friends made their homeward flight

All fell asleep without a fight

Older friends got a special treat

T'is the year Saint Nick, they'd meet

Growing up is so grand

Giving Santa a helping hand

Bo joined eight other crows

Tugging the moon with a big red nose

Bringing gifts so fast

Helping Santa complete his task

The End

Made in the USA
Columbia, SC
11 October 2021

46838525R00020